CHEATING EROTICA

Nice Guys

DON'T FINISH

LAST

JUST PLAIN BOB

WARNING

This book contains sexually explicit scenes and adult language. It may be considered offensive to some readers. This book is for sale to adults ONLY.

Please store your files wisely where they cannot be accessed by underage readers.

About the Publisher

4Fun Publishing, a member of **BLVNP Incorporated**, 340 S. Lemon #6200, Walnut CA 91789, info@blvnp.com / legal@blvnp.com
NOTE: Due to the highly emotional reaction of some people to works of erotic fiction, any email sent to the above address that contains foul language or religious references is automatically deleted by our anti-spam software and will not be seen. All other communications are welcome.

DISCLAIMER

Please don't be stupid and kill yourself. This book is a work of FICTION. Do not try any new sexual practice that you find in this book. It is fiction and not to be confused with reality. Neither the author nor the publisher or its associates assume any responsibility for any loss, injury, death or legal consequences resulting from acting on the contents in this book. Every character in this book is over 18 years of age. The author's opinions are not to be construed as the opinions of the publisher. The material in this book is for entertainment purposes ONLY. Enjoy.

Nice Guys Don't Finish Last

Cheating Erotica

By: Just Plain Bob

ISBN: 978-1-68030-580-7

I was sitting on the hood of the car parked in front of room 128 when the door opened and they came out. She saw me, and her face lost its color. Her eyes couldn't meet mine and she looked away. As I slid off the hood of the car, he put his hands up in a defensive gesture, and I said:

"Don't bother. Neither one of you is worth wasting my time on."

I walked over to my car, got in, and drove away. There was a long story that led up to that confrontation.

***

I met Jim when his family moved in to the house next door. He was eight, the same age as me, and the only other boy in the neighborhood. There were several girls close to my age, but Jim and I were the only boys. We naturally gravitated toward each other, and by the end of the fourth grade we were as tight as twin brothers. We played Little League baseball and Pop Warner football together. I had his back and he had mine. If you were messing with Jim you were messing with me, and vice versa. We were inseparable all the way through high school.

I met Laura when I started tenth grade and we started dating. By our junior year we were going steady. Jim had hooked up with Annabelle Spears and they were going on double dates with Laura and me. The night of the senior prom, Laura gave me her virginity in the room next door to where Jim and Annabelle were doing the same thing.

High school graduation broke us up. Jim had no interest in going to college so he joined the Navy. Annabelle called him every dirty name in the book for running off and leaving her, but even so she said she would wait for him to get a permanent duty station and then she would join him.

Laura and I went to college. Me to Eastern Michigan University for a degree in Civil Engineering, and Laura to University of Michigan for Information Technology. U of M in Ann Arbor and EMU in Ypsilanti were only a half hours drive apart, so Laura and I were still able to maintain a more or less steady relationship. I say 'more or less' because a couple of times Laura cancelled a date with me in order to go out with some guy she met at U of M—but of course she didn't tell me that part. I got that information from friends who also went to Michigan, and they also told me that she dated on the nights that I didn't drive over.

It came to a head one night when I drove over and got there just in time to see her get in a car with some guy and drive off. I followed them to a restaurant out on Ann Arbor Road, gave them ten minutes to get inside and get situated, and then I followed them in. I found them in a booth in the back—they were sitting side by side and not across from each other. He had his arm around her, and she was making no effort to push it off or move away and put some distance between them.

Luckily, there was a booth on the other side of the room where I could sit and where Laura couldn't miss seeing me. But it wasn't until the waitress asked me what I'd like to drink and Laura heard my voice that she looked my way. I was pretending to read the menu and was not looking right at her, but I saw her eyes get big, and she suddenly pushed the guy's arm off of her and moved away from him. The look on his face as she did those things said plain as day, "What are you doing?" That look told me that this wasn't the first time they had been together or even the second or third. They had been together enough that he felt comfortable putting his arm around her and he knew that she was okay with it.

I have no idea what they talked about, but Laura kept nervously looking my way while I sat there and pretended that I hadn't seen her. I finished my meal and then got up and left, without once letting Laura see me looking at her, and then I drove on home.

***

The next day was a Friday, and Laura and I had a standing date for dinner and a movie on Friday night. That Friday night, I skipped our date. I didn't call and cancel—I just didn't go. I unplugged the phone and settled in with a good book. Saturday I went to a party at the Delta Phi house and had a great time. I met a dark-haired beauty named Robin. We danced a couple of times and she gave me her number and asked me to give her a call.

Sunday I had my head in the books preparing for Monday's classes, when my doorbell rang. I got up, went to the door, looked through the spy hole, and saw that it was Laura. I opened the door and she pushed by me to enter the room, and then she turned to me and said:

"Where have you been? Where were you Friday night and why haven't you answered your phone?"

I closed the door, turned to her, and asked her which one she wanted me to answer first.

"What?"

"That was three questions. Which one do you want me to answer first?"

"Don't be cute, Rob. What is going on?"

"Okay then, I'll do them in the order that I like. First—where have I been. Here, for the most part, although I did go to a frat party Saturday night. Next—why haven't I answered the phone. That one is easy. I haven't answered it because it hasn't rung. My bad of course, since I am the one who unplugged it. Then there is "Where were you Friday night." I was here. I called out for a pizza and spent the evening reading a very good book."

"Why didn't you call me and let me know that you weren't coming over?"

"I figured that you already had something going with your boyfriend."

"My boyfriend? What are you talking about, Rob? You are my boyfriend."

"Oh? Well then who was that you were all lovey-dovey with at the restaurant Thursday night?"

"He is just a guy I know and we were not all lovey-dovey."

"Sitting next to you hip to hip, you leaning into him and his arm around you *isn't* lovey-dovey? What then would you call it?"

"It didn't mean anything, Rob. We are just friends."

"If you didn't think you were doing anything wrong, Laura, why didn't you get up and come over and say hi? How about maybe asking me to join you so you could introduce me to your friend? Maybe sit down with me and say a few words before going back to join your date? Could it be that you didn't do that because then he might want to know who I was and you didn't want to tell him?"

"Why didn't you get up and come over if it bothered you so much?"

"Because I wanted to see how you behaved."

"See how I behaved? Why would you want to do that?"

"Because I have too many people telling me about how much you date when I'm not around. I've also been told that you have been out with guys on nights you have broken dates with me. So yes, I wanted to see how you behaved with another guy."

"You don't own me, Rob. There isn't anything saying that we are exclusive."

"I thought there was, Laura. I seem to remember giving you my class ring and my letter sweater as signs that we were going steady."

"Letter sweater? Class ring? Going steady? Oh come on, Rob, that is just so high school."

"Maybe, but it happened in high school and when we left high school I don't recall you giving those things back to me and saying, 'We are out of high school now so all bets are off.' But that's okay. Since you don't feel like it binds you, I guess I can look at it the same way. I did meet a nice girl at that frat party and she did give me her phone number, so I guess I'm now free to give her a call."

Laura got a nasty look on her face and snapped out, "Fine! Go ahead for all I care," and she walked out. After she was gone I thought about how she hadn't made any excuses, hadn't said that she wouldn't do it again, and hadn't tried to convince me that I was her one and only. As far as she was concerned she wasn't a high school girl anymore—now she was a grown woman and things were going to be different, and that pretty much told me to write her off. It wasn't going to be an easy thing to do since we had been together for so long, but better to find out where her head was at now than later.

***

I had a ton of homework Monday, Tuesday, and Wednesday, so it was Thursday before I got a chance to call Robin. We talked for a while and then made a date for Friday night. I picked her up and we went and had dinner, and then instead of a movie she decided that she wanted to go to a party she knew about. It was at an apartment in Belleville and we got there just a little after eight.

And wouldn't you know that it just had to happen?

The first people I saw when we walked in the door were Laura and the guy she had been out with on Thursday night.

"Oh fuck!" I said.

"What's the matter?" Robin asked.

"Them," I said as I pointed to Laura and the guy. "You know them?"

"I know her."

"You know Miss Piggy?"

"*Miss Piggy?*"

"That's her nickname."

"Why does she have a nickname like that?"

"She's a slut. A real pig, so someone hung the Miss Piggy tag on her."

"Are you sure that she's a slut?"

"What else would you call a girl who has a steady boyfriend that she says she is going to marry and spends her time spreading for other guys when the boyfriend isn't around?"

"You know this for a fact? The spreading part, I mean?"

"No. To be fair about it, I don't know it personally, but I've heard it from several guys who said that they have played around with her."

"You didn't say how you knew her."

"I'm the boyfriend she was going to marry, right up until I caught her last Thursday with the guy she is standing with."

"Oh boy. Are there going to be any fireworks?"

"No. I had it out with her on Sunday. We are now officially toast."

"What are the chances that I would have heard from you if Thursday had never happened?"

"Slim next to none. But Thursday did happen and we came here to have a good time, so how about we get to it?"

She took my hand and led me through the room to introduce me to our host. Laura, who had been facing away from us when we walked in, caught sight of me and got a shocked expression on her face. Shocked because she never expected to see me at a party like that, or shocked because I'd caught her with her new boyfriend again—I didn't know. I ignored her as Robin led me over to a tall man standing with a tall blonde woman. She introduced me to Gary and his wife Ardis and we made small talk for a couple of minutes, and then Robin led me away to get us a drink.

The basement had been made into a recreation room and it was being used as a dance floor. Robin and I danced, had a few drinks, she introduced me to some people, and I had a great time. Every time I noticed Laura, she was looking at me with an expression on her face that I couldn't read.

Around eleven Robin said that it was time to leave because she had something pressing to do on Saturday, so we looked up our hosts and said our goodbyes. As I was driving Robin home, she said:

"Your ex seemed to spend a lot of time looking your way tonight."

"Probably was surprised at seeing me there."

"No, the feeling I got was that she wasn't at all happy seeing you with another girl."

"Tough shit. She was the one who caused me to end our relationship."

"Maybe, but I don't think that she is happy about it."

"Maybe not, but she is going to have to get used to it."

"Does that mean that I'm going to see more of you or that you are going to start dating all the ladies?"

"I'm a one girl at a time kind of guy. I enjoyed your company tonight and I'm going to ask you out again. Until you say no to my asking, you are my one girl."

"What if I'm not ready to be hanging with just one guy all the time?"

"Then you say no when I ask and I'll go looking for another girl to date. When she gets to the point where she says no, I'll give you a call and see how you are. If it is still no, I'll find a third girl and keep repeating the process until I find one who never says no."

"Well, I do like your attitude and I can see possibilities, so maybe we can give it a run."

"How about tomorrow night?"

"Sounds good."

I walked her to her door and said goodnight, and as I turned to leave she told me to wait a minute. I turned back to her and she said:

"I never kiss on the first date, but I guess there has to be a first time for everything," and she kissed me.

"See you tomorrow," she said as she went inside.

***

My dad was still up when I got home and he told me that Laura had called and that she had sounded upset. I told him that it was too late and that I'd do it in the morning.

As was my habit I slept in late on Saturday morning, and when I got up and got to the kitchen for my first cup of coffee, my mother told me that I needed to call Laura. "She has already called twice this morning."

"Not until I've had my first cup of coffee."

"Things not going well between you two?"

"Us two are no longer a two."

"Does she know that?"

"She should. She is the one who made the decision."

Just then the phone rang, and mom answered it and then said, "It is for you. It's Laura."

I took the phone and said, "Yes?"

"Why didn't you call?"

"It was too late to call when I got home last night and I just got out of bed this morning."

"I don't mean that. I mean why didn't you call me yesterday evening about picking me up for our regular Friday night date?"

"We hashed all that out last Sunday, Laura. You told me we weren't exclusive and you decided to date others. I told you that if it was good enough for you to date others then I would too, and you stormed out of the house."

"I didn't mean it, Rob. You should have known that."

"Don't give me that bullshit, Laura. You were already out with that clown I saw you with last Thursday."

"I was not out with him, Rob. I went to that party alone and he just happened to be there."

"Sure Laura, whatever you say. It doesn't matter anyway. I'm starting to hear all kinds of things about you and the things you have done. Things like how you got the nickname 'Miss Piggy'."

"I don't know what you've heard Rob, but it isn't true."

"Why wouldn't I believe that it's true after seeing you with your buddy at the restaurant? And I'm not buying that you just happened to accidently meet up with him at the party. He was standing way too close to you and had his arm around you when I walked into the party. No Laura, you aren't interested in sticking with just me and I'm not interested in being one of many. I would appreciate it if you would return my class ring and letter sweater. I realize that it is just too high school for an adult like you, and it doesn't seem to mean anything to you anyway. See you around. Goodbye."

"That sounded pretty final," my mom said.

"She decided that being my steady wasn't enough for her, and like I just told her, I'm not interested in standing in line."

***

I started keeping steady company with Robin, and about two months after we started dating we ended up in bed together, and it was then that I found out just how inexperienced I was. Laura and I had made love and it had been great, but it had been mostly all "plain vanilla" sex. Laura wouldn't let me eat her pussy and the most she would do where my cock was concerned was kiss it and then pull it in her. We made love often, but it was always in the missionary position, but as I said it was great so I went along with the flow.

Robin was vastly different. Much, much more experienced than I was—and she set out to correct my deficiencies. She sucked my cock and she swallowed. She wanted her pussy eaten before we made love and sixty-nine after to build me up for a second time. Missionary, cowgirl, reverse cowgirl, doggie, and something she called the "leg lift spoon" were the positions she favored. She liked sex in semi-public places where there was a chance of being discovered. She kept things exciting.

I would have to say that she pretty much owned me, but somewhere deep inside myself I knew that Robin and I had no long-term future, and that the day would come when she would cut herself loose from me. I hoped that it wouldn't happen, but I was still getting myself ready for it mentally.

Meanwhile, Laura made an effort to keep in touch. She sent me a card on Valentine's Day, and one on my birthday. She would call every couple of weeks just to say hi, ask how things were going at school, and how I was doing in my classes. I saw her from time to time at parties and she never seemed to be with the same guy twice. She would smile at me and give me a little wave, but she never tried to talk to me. Robin of course noticed, and would tell me that she could tell that Laura wanted me.

"But she ain't gonna get you, stud, 'cause you are mine and I don't share."

All I could do was smile and say, "Yes dear."

While all of that was going on, I was getting a letter from Jim about every two weeks or so, telling me about how things were going in his life. He had finished boot camp and had gone into specialty training. He was assigned to the Naval Construction Battalion otherwise known as the Seabees. He was learning to build things and tear things down. He never asked about Annabelle, so when I wrote back I never mentioned Annabelle either. Not that I would have anyway. He really wouldn't have liked hearing about what she was doing.

He hadn't been gone a week and Annabelle was putting out for some guy she met at a party. A month later he was gone and Annabelle was living with a guy she met where she worked, and three months later he was history and she was living with a black guy she met when he towed her car into the shop when it broke down. I don't know it for a fact, but I heard that he had her pulling trains for a bunch of his friends in his apartment.

And then suddenly Annabelle was gone, and no one had a clue as to where she had gone. At least not until I got a letter from Jim. He had finally finished training and was assigned to Norfolk as his permanent duty station. As soon as he was there he had sent for Annabelle and she had gone to join him.

"Wish you could have been here to be my best man, but we didn't have a lot of time to set things up. The sooner we could make it happen the sooner we could get on the list for base housing."

"Poor bastard," I thought. "First time you ship out she will have some other dude between her legs before the sound of the door closing behind you fades."

***

I wasn't hurting for money, since my grandparents had set up a college fund for me the day I was born. There was enough in it to pay for college and allow me to rent an apartment off campus if I wanted to, so at the start of my junior year Robin and I moved in together, and I started to get a taste of what married life would be like—I liked it. After living together for about six months I began to think about making it permanent. I still had that "itty-bitty" feeling that what I had with Robin was too good to be true, but Robin showed no sign of not wanting to continue our relationship.

That is she showed no sign, until the day I suggested that we go looking for an engagement ring. That was when she informed me that when she graduated she was going back to California, and would be marrying her childhood sweetheart who was currently in England on a Rhode's Scholarship. He knew all about me and she knew all about the English girl he was living with.

"We knew that there was no way two healthy young adults with high sex drives were going to go several years without sex, so we agreed on an open relationship. It shouldn't affect us in any way Rob, at least not right away. We still have a year before we graduate and leave."

But of course it did affect us, or *me* anyway. Basically what it amounted to was that I had just been taken from what I thought was a romantic relationship and had been placed in a fuck buddy relationship. The problem was that I just wasn't a fuck buddy kind of guy. I needed more than just sex out of a relationship and Robin and I slowly pulled apart. The sex was there when we went to bed at night, but the everyday interaction that takes place between couples became forced and strained.

Four months—almost to the day—from the day Robin put a stop to my romantic aspirations, she said to me:

"You don't really want to be here, do you?"

I told her that I was uncomfortable and I told her why.

"I'm sorry, lover. I almost wish that I didn't love Alex so much so I could be more of what you want. For what it is worth, if it wasn't for Alex, you would be my man."

"Thanks, I think."

"So what do we do? Flip a coin to see who stays and who goes?"

"No need. I knew this day was coming and my mom says she hasn't rented out my room yet. She figured that she better keep it available for me, at least until I turn forty or give her grandkids. So, you stay and I go."

"Friends?"

"Always."

She took me in her arms, gave me a kiss that made me weak in the knees, and then asked:

"One last night, please?"

***

I'd been back home for a week, and on Friday evening as I was in my room working on a paper due the next week, my mom called up the stairs:

"Rob? Someone's here to see you."

I went downstairs and found my mother talking to Laura. Mom looked at me and said:

"I'll leave you two alone," and she went into the kitchen.

"Hi Rob."

"Hello Laura. How have you been?"

"So so, but I'm hoping that things will get better."

"Oh?"

"Robin called me and told me that you were back on the market, and suggested that if I hurried I could be the first in line."

"Why would you want to be the first in line? Why would you want to be in line at all?"

"There wouldn't be a line if I hadn't gone stupid. In fact there never would have been a Robin. I don't want to be in line Rob; I just want to be back where I belong."

"Where you belong?"

She held up her left hand and said, "I never did give you your ring back."

On the ring finger of her left hand she was wearing my class ring.

"There is a party at Alice Johnson's house tonight. Would you like to take me?"

***

At the party, she hung all over me, and when I mentioned it she said, "Letting everyone know that I've staked my claim, baby. I've got you back and I'm letting everyone know it."

I'll admit it: it felt good to have Laura hanging on me again. The big surprise came after the party. When we pulled away from the curb in front of Alice's house, Laura slid over next to me and reached for my zipper. She worked my cock out and I expected that she was going to give me a hand job like she used to, but she bent down and took me in her mouth for the first time ever. I was so surprised I almost swerved off the road. In five minutes she had me ready to cum so I pulled over to the side of the road to let her finish me off. I told her I was going to cum so she could take her mouth off me and finish me by hand—but she stayed on me and swallowed when I spurted. She stayed with it until I went soft, and then she lifted her head and smiled at me:

"If you can't afford a motel, I'm good with the back seat."

I was immediately sorry that I'd given up the apartment to Robin, but luckily I had enough in my pocket for a motel room. The Laura that went into that motel room with me was not the same Laura that I had broken up with. She hurriedly stripped, and as soon as I had my pants and underpants off, she was on her knees in front of me working to bring me back to life. When I was up, she got on the bed on her hands and knees and said:

"Do me from behind baby—puppy fuck me."

She was surprised when I pushed her over on her back and then went down on her. I attacked her clit with lips and tongue until she cried out:

"No more baby, no more. I need you in me Robbie. Hurry baby, I need you."

I moved up on her and her legs came up and clamped on me as I pushed my way inside. She'd already gotten me off in the car so it took a while for me to cum again. On the way, Laura had two very noisy orgasms, and when I finally came and started to pull out she held me tight and wouldn't let me roll off of her. There were tears streaking on her cheeks and I asked her what was wrong.

"Nothing baby. I'm just happy. You're back, and I've got you, and I'm happy."

She finally let me loose and I settled onto the bed next to her. She curled into me and we laid there holding each other without saying a word for maybe five minutes, before I felt her hand move down my body, take hold of my limp cock and start fondling it. It twitched and she slid down and took it in her mouth for the third time that night. After a minute or so I pulled her into a sixty-nine, and we feasted on one another until she had my soldier at attention.

"Do me from behind this time, baby. Puppy fuck me. I love to puppy fuck. Puppy fuck me baby, puppy fuck me."

No, this was definitely the Laura that I used to know.

She was quiet as I drove her home. She just sat there and looked out the passenger side window. About halfway to her house she turned to me and said:

"I'm sorry, baby."

"About what?"

"About what we did tonight."

"Why are you sorry about that? I thought that it was pretty damned good."

"It was. What I am sorry about is that you weren't the first to do those things with me."

The truth was that I was pretty fucking pissed that I wasn't the first to do those things with her, but it was water under the bridge so I sucked it up and said:

"Don't forget that you didn't get to be the first one I got to do those things to either, but maybe it was for the best."

"How can you say that?"

"Just think back to where we were before. We made love for almost two years and never did any of the things we did tonight. I never even *thought* about doing those things. If we hadn't separated, would either of us have made any changes, or would we just have kept on doing it in the missionary position and never attempted something else? Robin was a very experienced young lady and she quickly taught me what I had to know to keep her happy. I'm not trying to pat myself on the back here, but I believe that I'm a much better lover now and it is likely that you can say the same. I wish that it had never happened, but it does seem that there was a benefit."

Laura gave me a thoughtful look, but she didn't say anything. When I pulled up in front of her house, I asked her if she wanted to go with me when I went apartment hunting on Saturday.

"An apartment is a whole lot cheaper in the long run than always having to use motels."

"Is that your way of asking me if I want to move in with you?"

"The thought did cross my mind."

"What time?"

"About nine."

"Okay. You have a date."

Laura and I moved into a two bedroom apartment about mid-way between Ann Arbor and Ypsilanti, and we turned the second bedroom into a study with a desk for Laura's computer and a desk for mine.

***

About a month after we moved in together Jim came home on a thirty day leave and he and Annabelle spent a lot of time with Laura and me. Jim and Annabelle seemed to be getting along great, so maybe I'd been wrong in the thoughts I'd had about her when she left.

Three weeks after Jim returned to duty, Annabelle showed up. Jim had shipped out to Iraq and Annabelle decided that she'd rather not wait at the base for Jim to return. She wasn't home two weeks and she was living with the guy she had been living with when she left to join Jim in Norfolk. Three weeks later she was seen with the black guy she used to date and rumors again started about the orgies she participated in at his apartment and the trains she pulled for his friends. I debated having a talk with her, but Laura talked me out of it. She told me that it wasn't any of our business and for all we knew, Jim and Annabelle had an open marriage.

"I've heard that it isn't uncommon in the service for both parties to agree that it is alright to play during long separations."

"That doesn't sound like something that Jim would go along with."

"So what are you going to do? Write and tell him? He worships the ground she walks on. He will not thank you for telling him that she is a slut. He will probably end up blaming you for being the one to ruin his life. Leave it alone, Rob."

***

Jim was back from Afghanistan in time to be the best man at my wedding to Laura and then he and Annabelle headed back for Norfolk where he finished out the last nine months of his enlistment. When he was discharged, he and Annabelle came home and he found a job with a construction company as a heavy equipment operator.

The next two years flew by and the Marshall's (Jim and Annabelle) were frequent guests at our place, and we went out with them at least once every two weeks or so. Things seemed to be great between Jim and Annabelle and there were no signs that she was cheating on Jim. Laura thought that maybe Annabelle was oversexed and needed it often, and so she was an easy lay when Jim wasn't around, but he was enough for her when he was home.

I guessed that was as good as explanation as any, and Laura's theory seemed to be born out when the company Jim worked for bid on and got a job doing some pipeline work in Alaska. The conditions on and around the site were harsh, so Jim decided to leave Annabelle at home for the four months he would be gone. Jim wasn't a week gone and Annabelle was seen going into a motel room with Gary Mellows, who was the owner of the company that Jim worked for, and after that Gary's vehicle was seen parked in Jim's driveway almost every night of the week. The job in

Alaska ran into some problems and the job was extended another two months.

Laura and Annabelle saw the same doctor and Laura just happened to be in the doctor's office the day that Annabelle got the bad news. She was seven weeks pregnant and Jim had been gone a little over three months. The way Laura found out was that two of the nurses that worked at the clinic had gone to school with us and knew that she knew Annabelle, and that she spent a lot of time around Annabelle. They asked her how she thought Jim would handle the news (patient confidentiality takes a back seat to spreading the dirt among friends) and Laura thought for a minute and then said:

"Jim will never know. If I'm right in what I'm thinking, Annabelle will abort, and it will all be over and done with before Jim gets home."

That isn't the way it went down.

Someone who didn't have a Laura to talk them out of it let Jim know what was going on. Jim flew home, rented a car, and parked down the street from his house until he saw Mellows pull in his drive, park and go into the house. He waited fifteen minutes to give Gary and Annabelle time to get down to it, and then he went into the house with a digital camera ready and caught the lovers in action. Fifteen minutes later the EMTs answered the 911 call and Mellows was carted off to the hospital.

The cops came and were going to haul Jim away until he showed them the pictures that he took. The camera was a Canon Rebel and Jim had it set to shoot continuously and the series clearly showed Mellows getting off Annabelle and charging at Jim. He probably was just trying to get to the camera and take it away from Jim, but given the way the series of shots came out, Jim was able to say that it was obvious that he was being attacked and he only defended himself. The cops bought it and left. Twenty minutes after the cops left, Annabelle was out on the front porch with one suitcase and the door was locked behind her.

The divorce was a slam-dunk, as was the suit filed against Mellows for alienation of affections. He also sued Mellows on some sort of sexual harassment thing, claiming that Mellows only hired him so he could send him out of town and then move in on his wife. Mellows could have settled out of court and avoided having everything become public, but he unwisely decided to fight, and as a result, everyone found out what he had been doing with an employee's wife after sending the employee out of town for a long period of time. The jury found for Jim and he was awarded one point three million. After legal fees and taxes, he ended up with just a little over seven hundred and fifty thousand. He paid off his house, put in an in ground swimming pool, and bought a new Ford F-350. Once the divorce was final, Annabelle dropped out of sight and the word was that she moved out of town.

Mellows had to sell off some equipment and property to settle the suit, and he lost a lot of business when some customers and potential customers decided that anyone who would do what he did with an employee's wife couldn't be trusted.

Jim still had some money left from his settlement, and he came to me and proposed that we form our own company and go after the business that Mellows lost out on. I would take care of the engineering and Jim would handle the construction end of the business. Laura and I talked it over, reviewed our finances, and decided to do it, and R and J Constructors was born as a partnership. We did well. We not only picked up a lot of the customers who left Mellows, but we underbid him on several jobs, and human nature being what it is, Jim made sure that everyone knew whenever we beat Mellows.

***

The next five years flew by. Jim played the field, but never found anyone he wanted to be tied to permanently. He spent a lot of time with Laura and me, and we went out on the average of once a week, with Jim and his date of the moment. The business was doing great. Laura had climbed the ladder at her company and was a regional manager, and the odds on favorite for the next VP opening. I didn't think things could get much better—and unfortunately, I was right.

It was a Tuesday and I was just leaving a lunch meeting with a prospective client when Gary Mellows came up to me and asked me if he could buy me a drink. I personally had nothing against Gary. My view was that if a cunt like Annabelle offered it up to a single guy like Gary, you couldn't really blame him for taking the gift. I never bought the story that Gary shipped Jim out of town to get Annabelle. I'd always known that Annabelle was a slut, so my take on it was that Annabelle probably did something like, go to Gary's office to pick up Jim's paycheck and had let Gary know that she was lonely with Jim being gone. Whatever, his problems were with Jim and not me, so I took him up on his offer to buy me a drink.

As soon as he sat down he asked, "How's business?"

"Not bad, but could be better."

"Would you consider selling?"

"Selling? Why would I want to do that?"

"To stick your buddy Jim with me for a partner."

"Are you smoking some kind of bad shit?"

"Not really. I hate to be the one to do this, but have a look at these."

He opened his briefcase, took out a folder, and handed it to me. I picked it up, opened it, and was stunned. The first thing I saw in the folder was a picture of Laura and Jim holding hands as they walked into a motel room. There were several others of the two of them going into or coming out of motel rooms, and another half dozen in various places kissing and hugging. There was one photo of them kissing on the back seat of Laura's car. They could have done that on the front seat, so you didn't have to be a genius to figure out what they were getting ready to do or had just finished doing. I looked up at Gary and he said:

"I'm sorry. I've had him watched so I could get something on him so I could get back at him. When the PI brought me these pictures I didn't know she was your wife. I could tell from the rings in the pictures that she was somebody's and I set the PI on her to find out who she was so I would have the information when I started to get my payback."

"Why? You were guilty. You did what he said you did."

"No I didn't. Yes, I did have an affair with his wife, but I never sent him out of town so I could get to her. She walked into my office, locked the door behind her, and started taking off her clothes. She looked me right in the eye and said:

"You sent Jim out of town so you have to take care of me until he gets back."

"I'm single and I love pussy as much as any other guy so am I going to say no to a naked Annabelle? As far as I'm concerned, the whole mess was Jim's fault to begin with. Everyone knows that Annabelle is a slut and has been one since high school. Jim had to know. He had to know and he never did anything about it. No Rob, he fucked me with that law suit and I'm going to get him back. I'm just sorry that you ended up in the middle of it."

"Any idea of how long it has been going on?"

"The PI says from what he has been able to find out it has been at least a year and probably longer."

"How in the fuck could it have gone on for that long and me not find out?"

"If she never did anything to make you suspicious how could you have known?"

"So why do you want to buy me out? What do you gain by being Jim's partner?"

"Think about it. As an equal partner I have an equal say. He says we need to do A and I say no, we have to do B. It doesn't matter what he wants I'm going to be 180 degrees away. Plus I'll know what we are bidding on jobs and I'll make sure that my other company bids lower. I'll ruin the company and Jim will lose his ass."

"But so would you?"

"Not really. I've checked it out. If the business fails, we sell off the assets and I get a good portion of my money back. I won't make money, except of course what I make from my other company when I underbid the jobs Jim bids on, but I won't lose all that much either."

"What if he decides to just stomp your ass every morning to start his day out right until you've had enough and sell your half to him or someone else?"

"Last time he caught me on top of his wife and all I could think about was getting that camera away from him. He got in three good shots before it dawned on me that I should be defending myself and not worrying about that stupid fucking camera. He won't have it that easy if he tries it again. In fact, I'm pretty sure that I can take him if it comes to that. So, you interested?"

"I just might be, but first, I want to do some digging of my own."

"If you do decide, do you have a ballpark of what you will want?"

I gave him a figure, and he said that it might be doable and to give him a call if I decided to do it.

***

I left the meeting with Mellows with my mind in turmoil. How the hell could Laura and Jim have been doing it behind my back for almost a year, and me not have even the remotest suspicion? I'd seen absolutely nothing to indicate that Laura was dissatisfied with me. I'd seen no loss of affection. Our sex life was still great—at least I thought it was. Three, sometimes four times a week, and with plenty of foreplay. We cuddled on the couch while watching TV and she slept up against me every night. She never walked by me without touching me. She was like a teenager when we were in the car; always sliding over to be next to me.

What went wrong?

I had no reason to doubt the report and photos from Gary's detective, but photos could be doctored, and Gary did have an agenda. I wanted to be dead certain before I took action, so I went back to the office, called a friend who worked for an insurance agency, and asked him who they used to investigate suspicious claims. Armed with that information, I called and made an appointment, and thirteen days later I had my certainty. On Wednesdays when Jim was supposedly out visiting job sites, he was actually meeting Laura at the Comfort Inn on Melrose. How she managed to get off work for their meetings, I had no idea.

All that was left was for me to decide what to do. Actually, I knew what I wanted to do, but I needed to find a way to make it work. Two hours with an attorney got me a list of things I could do and couldn't do, and a list of things I *should* do. We were a no fault state and so everything would have to be split equally between us. My concern was going to be avoiding giving her a dime of what I realized from the sale of my half of the company. I finally had to accept that the only way I could do that was lie. Even then, she would still get some of it.

I made the deal with Mellows to sell him my share of the company on paper for a third of what he actually paid. That third went into a bank account in my name only. The other two thirds went to an offshore account that I set up. The deal was that he wouldn't show up at the office and take over my desk until the morning after I served Laura and Jim with the papers: Laura for a divorce on the grounds of adultery, and Jim for alienation of affections. Even though we were in a no fault state I could still sue for adultery, and depending on the judge we drew, it could mean a little better split than fifty-fifty.

In order for the adultery grounds to fly, I needed proof. A review of the reports from Gary's PI and mine showed that every time they were under observation, they used the same motel and it was always on a Wednesday. My detective rented a room and set it up to record the action, and a healthy bribe to the desk clerk insured that they would be put into that room.

Wednesday morning I called Maria, our receptionist, and told her to tell Jim I would not be in that morning because of a dentist appointment.

"And tell him if I don't feel all that good after the tooth is pulled I might not even be in this afternoon."

"You got it, boss. If I were you, I would go home and rest. I've never had a tooth pulled yet that didn't hurt like hell when the laughing gas wore off."

I left the house and circled back after Laura left for work. The locksmith was there at nine changing all the locks on the house. As soon as he was done, I drove over to the bank and cleaned out the accounts and safe deposit box. My attorney said to only take half, but my mood was stone-assed, "Fuck you Laura," and I wasn't going to do anything that would make it easy on her. She'd get her half eventually, but only after she'd had to fight for it. I also withdrew the funds I thought I had coming from the business. If it was too much, Jim could go to court and try and get it back, but as long as I had it, he wouldn't.

My detective called me at twelve ten and told me that the happy couple had arrived and were in room 128. I drove over and had a few words with my detective, and then I sat on the hood of the car parked in front of the room and waited until they came out.

***

After the mini confrontation I got in my car and drove off. As I pulled away, a man got out of a car and walked up to them and served them. In with the divorce papers that Laura received was a temporary restraining order keeping her 500 feet from me and the house. I had to fudge things a little to get it. I had to lie and say that I had been told by a third party that Jim and Laura had been overheard discussing how much life insurance I had, and wondering how much my share of the business would be worth. There would be a hearing on whether or not to make it permanent, but that could take a couple of weeks. It was just one more way to fuck over Laura. The big thing was that she couldn't come into the house without someone from the court being there and I didn't plan on making myself available to furnish the keys to the new locks.

In with Jim's papers on the alienation of affections suit was a short note. It said:

"You know how these suits work, right? How does it feel to be on the other end of one?"

As I drove away from the motel, I gave Gary a call on my cell. "It is done. Have a great first day tomorrow at the office."

***

I drove to the airport, parked the car in the long term lot, tossed my cell phone into the glove compartment, and caught a flight to Cabo San Lucas. I spent a week scuba diving and lying on the beach, and then I flew home.

My cell was loaded with voice mails when I turned it on. Not surprisingly, most were from Laura, but there were four from Jim. I would have thought I'd be the last person he would want to talk to. No matter—I had no interest in speaking to him or Laura. Would I have liked an explanation? Of course I would like to know why, but I'd made up my mind to put the two of them behind me and get on with my life. The 'why' of their betrayal was something that I didn't need my mind to be carrying around.

My attorney knew that I was going to be gone for a week so I decided to call him and let him know I was back. He asked me to call Laura and let her know I was back. She had been calling him twice a day trying to get in touch with me so she could get into the house and get some of her things. I was on the verge of telling him to call her and set up something with the court to get her into the house supervised—when I had a thought. One more way to fuck over her. I called her and asked her what she wanted.

"I need to get my clothes and other things, but I can't get in even with someone from the court because I don't have a key and the people from the court won't let me break in."

"You don't have anything there to pick up. I gave it all to Goodwill. I didn't want anything of yours in the house to remind me of your lying, cheating ass. There isn't anything of yours here anymore, not even a stray hair pin."

"Damn it Rob, you had no right to do that!"

"I had as much right to do that as you had to stab me in the back."

"We need to talk Rob. It isn't what you think."

"Get real Laura. I don't *think* you were fucking Jim; I *know* it for a fact. Goodbye, Laura."

I hung up on her. All of her stuff was still in the house, but again, fucking over her is what I wanted to do. Eventually she would get her things, but it wasn't going to be anytime soon.

***

I'd always been on good terms with Maria who was our receptionist, secretary, bookkeeper, chief cook, and bottle washer so I gave her a call and asked how things were going.

"Not bad for me, but not so good for the company. Nothing is getting done. Gary and Jim constantly argue over the least little thing. Jim says do something and then Gary says don't do it. Jim will call and order something, and as soon as Jim is out of the office, Gary will call and cancel the order. We have jobs to start, but they just sit there as Jim and Gary go at it. I got so fed up I gave my notice last Friday, but Gary told me he would double my wages if I would stay, so naturally I'm not going to leave.

"The two of them did get into a fist fight on Thursday, but outside of beating the hell out of each other, there wasn't a winner, although Jim did get a broken nose out of it. Why did you bail out on us? Why did you sell out to Gary?"

I told her the story behind it and she was silent for a minute, and then she said:

"Now I've got another reason to stay."

"What's that?"

"I can help Gary. I've never liked Jim. He was always hitting on me even though he knew I was engaged. One time, he even hinted that he would let me go if I didn't go out with him and we both know what he meant when he said 'go out with.' I asked him what you would have to say about his letting me go and that shut him up."

"You should have told me."

"Why? It was a personal problem and I handled it. I'm sorry about you and Laura, Rob, but there could be a bright side to it, at least for me."

"How is that?"

"It means that you are back on the market. How do you feel about being chased after?"

"I thought you were engaged?"

"I was, until I caught the asshole doing to me what Laura was doing to you."

"When did this happen?"

"About three weeks ago."

"Well sweetie, for what is worth, I will put your name at the head of the list for when I start dating again, but it won't be for a while. I'm not going to give Laura anything that she can use against me."

"I can wait, but keep me in mind if you get lonely and would like a dinner date for company."

"I will sweetie, and thanks."

My phone rang sixteen times that day. Fourteen were from Laura and two were from Jim. I couldn't, for the life of me, think of what the asshole could want to say that I would want to hear, and if he was calling to ask for something he damned sure wasn't going to get it from me.

I deleted all the calls and went on home. I made myself some dinner, and then on a whim I called Gary Mellows and asked him how his plan was working.

"Not bad, not bad at all. I made sure that I was sitting at your desk when he came to work. He saw me and got a scowl on his face, and then asked me what the fuck I was doing in the office, sitting at your desk. I laughed at him and told him I was his new partner. The look on his face was *priceless*. You could almost see the steam coming out of his ears as he read a copy of our agreement. I got us off to the right start almost right away. He called for a fuel truck because the front end loader and some of the other equipment on the Wilkin's site where low on diesel. As soon as he left the office, I called and cancelled the order. One of the skid steers ran out of fuel and Jim got on the phone to Allied and cussed them out, and they told him that I had cancelled the order, that they did have to take that kind of crap from him, and for him to get his fuel from someone else. Then he came to me and asked me what the fuck I thought I was doing. I told him that Allied was charging us too much and that I was shopping around for a better price. And things went downhill from there."

"A little birdie told me that the two of you engaged in some fist-a-cuffs."

"Yeah. Things came to a head last Thursday."

"How did that work out?"

"I guess I was a little optimistic when I told you that I thought I could take him, but I held my own and I did hurt him."

"Well, carry on and good luck with your plan."

After hanging up, I went into the room I had converted into an office, fired up the computer, and began typing a resume. I'd start job hunting the next day. I was busy banging away on the keyboard when the doorbell rang. I opened the door to find Jim standing there.

"What the fuck do you want?"

"We need to talk Rob."

"No we don't, asshole."

"It wasn't my fault, Rob. She came after me. She caught me when I was in a really down mood over what Annabelle did to me. I wasn't thinking straight Rob. I'm sorry Rob, but it wasn't my fault. I didn't go after her."

"But you did know that she was my wife. You knew how you felt when you found out about Annabelle. And you didn't even stop for a second to think that you were going to make me feel the same way, did you? You had to know that I'd find out sooner or later, probably the same way you found out about Annabelle. Somebody told you. Well shitface, someone did tell me. You are a sack of shit as far as I'm concerned. You were supposed to be my friend and even if I believed that Laura made a move on you—which I don't—you should have turned away from her that same way I turned away from Annabelle when she made a move on me. You knew better, but you did it anyway. And even if it is true that she made the move and caught you when you weren't thinking straight, that doesn't excuse the second, third, fourth, and however many times that there were after that. No man—you stabbed me in the back and there isn't any getting past that."

"So why didn't you just whip my ass? Why did you saddle me with Mellows?"

"Because the mood I was in when I found out and the rage I felt. If I'd have come after you, I would probably have killed you, and you are not worth going to prison over. Besides, sticking you with Mellows will cause you grief that will last a whole lot longer than the effects of any beating. But you know what? The rage I felt then is gone."

And then I hit him. I caught him a good one on the chin and he started to fold. I grabbed the front of his shirt, pulled him into the house, kicked the door shut behind me, and then I stomped the hell out of him. He was unconscious when I dragged him out of the house and stuffed him into his car. You would not believe how big a smile I had on my face when I walked back into the house. I might get a visit from the cops, but I wasn't worried about it. All I had to do was say that he had attacked me and I defended myself; point to his fight with Mellows and say that he was pissed at me because I had sold my half of the business to Mellows, and he was trying to make me pay for it.

***

The next morning, I sent off fourteen resumes and then called my attorney to see what the status was. He told me that the coming Monday we had a hearing on the temporary restraining order, but he had not received any feedback from Laura or an attorney on her behalf. I debated calling Laura, but decided against it. The longer it went before she got an attorney, the longer it would be before I had to give her anything.

During the week I received several responses to the resumes I'd sent out. Wednesday I flew to Atlanta for an interview and Thursday found me in Baltimore. I felt good about both interviews, but I'd also had a response from a company in San Diego and I thought that I might just like living in a place where it was almost always warm, so I called and scheduled an interview for the following Tuesday.

Monday was the hearing on the temporary restraining order, and to the surprise of no one, the judge did not see any justification for leaving it in place and I was ordered to give Laura access to the house. Laura was of course at the hearing and she had a lawyer with her. She came up to me and started to say something, and I walked away from her, got my attorney, and then walked back to her.

"You don't say anything to me unless my attorney is present."

"All I was going to say is that I'll be over this evening."

"No, you won't. I'm flying out for a job interview at two-thirty and I won't be home until Wednesday. You can come by any time after six."

Her attorney started to say something but I cut him off. "She will not, and I repeat—will *not*—be in that house unless I'm there to monitor everything that she does."

"There will be someone from the court there to keep things above board and you can also have someone from your attorney's office there."

"Nope. Won't work. They would have no idea about what she was helping herself to. All they would do is list it and if it was something she wasn't supposed to have I'd end up having to fight to have it returned. She hasn't been in the house for two weeks and she has survived. Another forty-eight hours won't kill her."

Her attorney shook his head 'no' and said, "Then I guess we will have to see what the judge says," and he turned to go back and see the court clerk, but Laura stopped him.

"Just drop it," she said, "I can wait another forty-eight hours."

I looked at her and said, "Wednesday at six," and I turned to leave.

"Wait a second Rob. Can we talk then?"

"No," I said and then I walked out of the building.

***

I thought the interview in San Diego went well and I headed home hoping to hear from them. Laura arrived right at six with someone from her attorney's office. The woman from the court arrived at twenty to six and we spent the twenty minutes drinking coffee and talking. She told me that her job was just to observe for the court and inventory the items removed. She also would make a list of the disputed items and I told her that it wouldn't be necessary.

"She can have whatever she wants."

"If that is the way you feel, why have you taken such a hard line on things where she is concerned?"

"She stabbed me in the back and she did it with the man who had been my best friend for over twenty-five years. I couldn't beat her and I couldn't kill her—at least I couldn't if I wanted to stay out of jail—but I had to do something to get back at her and make her suffer. It wasn't much, but at least it was something."

Then the doorbell rang and I let Laura and the person she had with her from her attorney's office in, and I went outside to cut the grass. When I finished and came back in the house, everyone was gone except Laura, and she was sitting at the kitchen table nursing a cup of tea. She looked up at me when I came in.

"You lied to me. You didn't give any of my things to Goodwill."

"Maybe not, but I sure as hell enjoyed the outrage in your voice when you told me that I had no right to do it."

"I wasn't expecting it all to be here and it is going to take me longer to get it out than I expected."

I pulled my key ring out of my pocket, took a house key off of it, and slid it across the table to her. "Don't bother moving it. You can have the house on Friday. I'll have all of my things out of here by then."

"Why?"

"I'm interviewing for jobs and I'll be moving out of state as soon as I find one."

"I mean, why have you done what you have done if you were just going to give me the house and leave? Why the restraining order and lying to me about giving my things away?"

"That's a stupid question. After what you did to me, I had to do something to get back at you. Just be thankful that I decided to do it in a peaceful manner instead of a violent one. Fucking over you doesn't even come close to making us even, but it was the best I could so and still stay out of jail."

"I know you said no when I asked if we could talk tonight, but I am still going to try and convince you that we don't need to get divorced."

"Get serious, Laura. There is no way on this green Earth that we can stay together after what you did."

"But it didn't mean anything, Rob. I love you and you know it. What happened with Jim was a mistake—just a stupid mistake. I like Jim. I've always liked him, but I don't love him and I never have loved him."

"I don't give a shit if you loved him or not. You still fucked him, and love or just like, it was still infidelity, and there shouldn't be any doubt in your mind on how I feel about that. All you have to do is remember how upset I was over what Annabelle was doing to Jim. I was so upset I was going to let him know but I let you talk me out of it. That should have clued you in right there as to how I would take it if you did it to me. And don't give me any of that 'I never meant for you to find out' shit. Cheaters always get caught. Sooner or later they always get caught. Jim found out about Annabelle because someone saw her fucking around on him and told him. That's the same way you got caught. Someone saw you and Jim go into a motel room and they told me."

"Doesn't it even matter that I love you?"

"No, Laura, it doesn't, because it wasn't enough to keep you from cheating on me."

"But it didn't mean anything, Rob. Honest to God it meant nothing. It was an accident."

"An accident? How was fucking the man who used to be my best friend an accident?"

"He stopped by the house when you were on that trip to Santa Fe and he was in a downer of a mood over Annabelle. He really loved her, and even though he had thrown her out of his life, he was missing her. We had several drinks and after a while he started crying, and I took him in my arms, hugged him, and tried to comfort him. To this day I don't know how we ended up naked on the couch having sex, but we did—and even though I hate to admit it, it was great. There wasn't any love involved; it was just wild rutting sex, but it was exciting. I remember thinking that, 'This is just so wrong. I shouldn't be doing this, but it feels so good.' After, I figured out that it was the illicit nature of what we had done that made it so exciting. It was a turn on to cheat.

"The next time you went out of town Jim stopped over. We both knew why he was there and we did it again. I had a huge orgasm, but it wasn't because of the way Jim made love to me. It was because the cheating was such a turn on, and yes, I'll admit a good part of the turn on was because I was doing it with your best friend.

"There was no love involved, Rob. As trite as it may sound, it was just sex, Rob. Just some excitement added to my life. I never shorted you while it was going on. I love you, Rob. I really do and you know it. We can get by this. We don't need to get a divorce."

"'We' doesn't enter into it, Laura. I need a divorce. I can't live with someone who has betrayed me. It is just that simple, Laura. You betrayed me. If I kept you, I would spend the rest of my life watching you like a hawk and waiting for you to do it again. By your own admission you kept doing it because cheating was such a turn on. How long would it be before you remembered how great the orgasms were when you were cheating on me? How long before you decided that you wanted to experience those great orgasms again? You can promise me all you want that you will never do it again, but your promises aren't worth spit. You already promised me to 'forsake all others' when we got married and you broke that promise.

"I can't believe anything you say, Laura. Jim's story about how it happened doesn't even come close to yours. According to Jim it didn't 'accidentally' happen. According to him you made a play for him. He could be lying, or *you* could be. The problem is that after what the two of you did, neither one of you is trustworthy, as far as I'm concerned, so I can't pick one story over the other. The bottom line, Laura, is that we are done as a couple."

"I'm not giving up, Rob. I'll fight the divorce. I know we can get by this because we love each other. You are pissed at me right now, and justifiably so, but I can promise you and keep that promise especially now that I can see what breaking that promise can cost me. My attorney says that he can get the court to order counseling and I know that can help. I love you, Rob, and I'm not letting you go."

"You can't seem to understand that I don't want you now. Okay, I'll admit that I still love you and it is going to take me a while to get by this, but there is no fucking way that I can ever live with you again. Every fucking time I got in bed with you I would think of you with that asshole that used to be my best friend, and I won't live like that. You won't fight the divorce, Laura, because if you do I'll release the video I have of your last meeting with Jim. Every family member, every friend, and all of your co-workers will get a copy. I'll build you your own porn web site and there are dozens of amateur porn sites where I can post it, and I'll do it with your full name and address attached. It should make your life very interesting."

"Bullshit, Rob. No such video exists."

"Oh no? Wait right here."

I went into the den where I had my briefcase, took out a copy of the CD, went back into the kitchen and handed it to her.

"Check it out. After you have watched it, you decide if you want anyone else to watch it. Now, if you don't mind, I have things to do. You can have the house on Friday, but for now, you need to go.

On Thursday and Friday I moved out of the house and put most of my things in storage. Then I took a room at The Executive Suites for a month, expecting by the end of that time I would have a job.

***

During the next two weeks I made trips to Salt Lake City, Philadelphia, Atlanta, Chicago, and Detroit for interviews and I felt good about all of them, but I wasn't hearing back from any of them. I sat down and figured out my finances, and decided that I could make it for about six years without a job. I started checking out other cities and states for places with a lower cost of living; a cost of living that would allow me to stretch those six years to eight or maybe even ten.

Laura signed the divorce papers and returned them to my attorney. I was almost sorry that she did. I would have very much liked to have spread the CD of her and Jim all over the place, but a deal was a deal. I made out on the agreement. The agreement was a fifty-fifty split of assets, with each party paying their own attorney's fees. I was the one who filed so I paid the court costs. Laura said she wanted the house, and my half of the equity was just a little over what I had taken out of the bank, so that was a wash. I did have to give Laura half of what I'd gotten on the sale of my half of the company, but I knew that would happen and I had planned for it. She did bitch that I'd sold out too cheaply, but it didn't matter because the other two thirds of what I got from the sale were safely hidden.

An interesting thing came to me through the grapevine. It seems that once I took myself out of the picture, Jim went after Laura and was so persistent that she had to take out a restraining order against him. Not that I cared of course, but I did get a laugh out of it.

***

I decided to wait for the divorce to become final before making a move. I finally started hearing from some of the companies I had interviewed with. The company in San Diego called and asked me to come back out and talk with them, but before I could call and set it up, I got a call from Gary Mellows.

"How would you like your company back?"

"Why would I want the company back? I sold it to you to get back to Jim and get away from him. Why would I want to go back to being his partner?"

"You wouldn't, but then you wouldn't have to. After our last blow up I said, 'If you are so fucking unhappy with me as a partner, I'll buy you out or go sell your half to someone else.' He spent all of thirty seconds thinking about it and then asked me how much I'd give for his half. He took half of what I gave you."

"Still, the question is why would I want it back? If you did half of what you told me you were going to do to fuck over Jim, the company probably isn't worth all that much anymore."

"You might be surprised. Come on down to the office and let's talk."

I didn't figure that I had anything to lose so I went down to talk with him. When I walked in the door Maria jumped up from behind her desk, hugged me, and then stuck her head in the office door and told Gary that I was there.

"As you know, I only bought you out so I could fuck over Marshall. I didn't really want it and I had no real use for it. But things change. I am getting more and more into the construction end of the business. I want to get away from the engineering aspect. For one thing, I haven't been able to get what I wanted in the way of engineers, so I started thinking about what to do. The solution that came to me was to call you and ask you to set up a company that I contract to do my engineering, but then Marshall sold out to me and I thought why not just sell you back the company and contract with you."

"I can't afford to buy back my half and Jim's half."

"You don't have to pay that much because the company isn't worth that much anymore. Since I own the whole shebang, I transferred all of the construction work and construction equipment to my other company. All I'm leaving is the pure engineering part. I'll sell you the company for what I paid Jim and I'll sign a five year contract for engineering services, plus the company still has contracts with about fifteen other firms. I don't see how you can lose."

"How much did you give Jim?"

He told me and it was less than I had in my offshore account.

"There is one provision though."

"What would that be?"

"I have no secrets from Maria and I sounded her out on the idea. She told me that if you took it, she would be staying with you and not moving over to my company. If you take the deal, you are going to be stuck with her."

I didn't need to think too hard on it and I told him that I would take the deal, but to be on the safe side I wouldn't do it until my divorce was final, and that wouldn't be for another three weeks. Gary said that would work for him and we shook on the deal.

As I was leaving the office, Maria said, "I heard. Don't forget that when those three weeks are up, you promised that I would be first on the list."

"I didn't think you were serious about that."

"You can just bet that I am," she said with a thousand-watt smile.

As I pulled away from the curb, my cell rang and it was my attorney. Jim had learned a lesson from seeing what happened to Gary when Gary had fought Jim's suit against him, and he had called my attorney with an offer to settle. I told the attorney to take it. The rest of the drive to my room at the Executive Suites was made with a huge smile on my face. In three weeks I could start a new life, complete with a new job, a new girlfriend, and money in the bank. I could fill those three weeks looking for a place to live and shopping for furniture. Who says that nice guys always finish last?

~~The End~~

Here is a sample from another story you may enjoy!

Maeve and ROB
and

SHARING LOVERS EROTICA
JUST PLAIN BOB

It is my fault and I accept it. I don't try to blame anyone else. I allowed it to happen and up to the point where it went bad I was an active participant. If I blame it on anything, it would have to be love.

I fell head over heels in love with Maeve the first time I laid eyes on her. It was at a cocktail party that my company was throwing for our customers and suppliers. I was talking with the sales rep for the company that sold us some of the chemicals we use in our manufacturing process when she walked into the room. She was on the arm of a man I took an instant dislike to. Had never met, had never spoken to him, had never even heard of him, but my dislike was intense because she was with him and not me.

She was a fairly tall woman, maybe five foot seven or eight. Dirty blond hair that hung down below her shoulders. Very nice looking body, but I have to admit that I didn't spend much time trying to figure out her weight or measurements. It was her face that grabbed my attention. I don't know how to describe it. Her face had planes and angles. She looked an awful lot like porn star Krystal Summers. I couldn't take my eyes off of her. Suddenly there was a hand in front of my face, fingers snapping and a voice saying:

"Earth to Rob, Earth to Rob, come in please."

Charlie, the sales rep I had been talking to, chuckled and said:

"Obviously nothing that I have to say is going to register on you as long as she is in the room so I'll let you go. Call me in the morning."

Then he laughed and said, "Good luck" and walked toward the bar leaving me standing there staring at Maeve.

I was still staring at her when she turned her head and our eyes met. I felt a jolt all the way to the soles of my feet. She didn't smile at me or nod an acknowledgement; she held my eyes for a couple of seconds and then looked away. I spent the rest of the cocktail party watching her and making note of who she talked with so I could approach them later and in talking with them hopefully find out more about her.

I was standing at the bar waiting for the barmaid to build me a vodka tonic with lime when she walked up to stand next to me. She ordered a Cosmo and then turned to me and said:

"Do I have a big, nasty looking spot on my skirt or something like that?"

"Not that I noticed. Why?"

"Because every time I look your way you are looking at me."

Not being one to pass up an opening I said, "And at your age this comes as a surprise? You know you are drop dead gorgeous and that men, me among them, are going to be fascinated with you. I've spent most of the evening since you walked in trying to think of a way to meet you."

"Coming up to me and saying hello would work."

"I know, but it would be socially awkward since you are here with another guy."

"Why would it be awkward? You wouldn't say "Hello, I'd like to take you to bed," would you?"

"Of course not, but your date would know that my real purpose in coming up to you would be to try and separate you from him and that is what would make the situation awkward."

"Well fortunately for you he is just a date and he is replaceable and I just happen to have a soft spot for guys who find me fascinating."

She stuck out her hand and said, "Maeve Billings and I'll give you advance warning that I hate being called Mae."

I took her hand and carried it to my lips and lightly kissed it and said, "Rob. Rob Daltry."

"Nice meeting you, Rob. Although my date is replaceable he is still my date this evening and I need to get back to him." She started to walk away and then turned back to me.

"I'm in the book, Rob Daltry."

She turned and walked back to her date.

The next evening I called her and asked her to have dinner with me on Friday and she said she would love to.

If you enjoyed this sample then look for **Maeve and Rob**.

Also by this Author:

The Prodigal Family: The Abbotts

Watching My Shared Wife

The Waitress and the Runaway Husband

Baiting Mr. Little

Too Hot for Henry

Chuck's Fantasy

The Redhead's Desires

Rescued at Riley's

His Every Fantasy

Open Mike Night

Pursuit for Revenge

Why Does He Do That?

Halloween & Drugs

Tracey

When Rob Met Kari

Becoming a Shared Wife, Vol. 1 –

(Wife Sharing and Other Adventures)

Becoming a Shared Wife, Vol. 2 –

(Hazardous Wives)

Becoming a Shared Wife, Vol. 3 –

(Wives Who Stray)